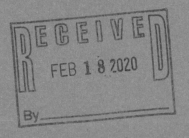

The Blunders
A Counting Catastrophe!

For Iliana, Verena, Eoin, Leonora, Beatrice, Elowyn,
Lucia, Aven, Mae, Neave, Anne Louise, and Hudspeth.
Did I forget anyone?
C. S.

To my three blunders:
Michelle, Gabriel, and Eli
C. J.

Text copyright © 2020 by Christina Soontornvat. Illustrations copyright © 2020 by Colin Jack. All rights reserved. No part of
this book may be reproduced, transmitted, or stored in an information retrieval system in any form or by any means, graphic,
electronic, or mechanical, including photocopying, taping, and recording, without prior written permission from the publisher.
First edition 2020. Library of Congress Catalog Card Number 2019939817. ISBN 978-1-5362-0109-3. This book was typeset in Dolly.
The illustrations were created digitally.
Candlewick Press, 99 Dover Street, Somerville, Massachusetts 02144. visit us at www.candlewick.com.
Printed in Shenzhen, Guangdong, China. 19 20 21 22 23 24 CCP 10 9 8 7 6 5 4 3 2 1

The Blunders
A Counting Catastrophe!

Christina Soontornvat   illustrated by Colin Jack

CANDLEWICK PRESS

BLESS THIS MESS

It wasn't even lunchtime and the ten Blunder children were driving their mother up the wall.

They'd blundered the laundry.

They'd blundered the bathtub.

They'd let the hamsters out and the dog in, and the entire house was one giant blundered-up disaster.

Their mother's ears were the color of a ripe tomato.
"That's enough! Go play outside and give me some peace!"

"Yes, Mother!"

"And keep track of each other!"

"We will!"

"I want all ten of you home by sunset!"

"We promise!"

The children played outside for hours in the cool of the creek, where there wasn't much they could blunder up.

It was getting late when they finally remembered their promise to their mother.

"Everybody line up!" said Betty. "Time to do a head count!"

"Let me do it," said Brenda. "You've got to tap everyone on the head as you're counting. Like this."

"Let me handle this," said Bernice.

Raise your hand if you're lost.

Hmmm . . .

Bonnie counted by threes.

It was no use. No matter what they did,
they only came up with nine.

The sun was setting. The sky was turning red.
It made them think of their mother.

"But what are we going to tell her?" wailed Bess.

"Everybody just keep cool," said Barnaby.

"Let's tell her that one of us had to attend an important business meeting and will be home shortly," said Ben.

This sounded like a very good idea.

By the time they walked in the door, their mother's ears were as red as boiled beets. "Where on earth have you been?"

The children started to spin more tales about the business meeting, but when they saw ten plates set out lovingly on the dinner table . . .

Their mother put her hands on her hips.
She looked down at her weeping children . . .

and hugged them up.

"Would you look at that," she said softly.
"I think I may have found the tenth one."

To prove it, she counted each of them with a kiss:
Bruce, Betty, Ben, Bill, Brenda, Beau, Bonnie, Bess, Bernice, and Barnaby.

That night after dinner, their mother held up two empty pie tins.
"What happened to all the pie?"

"We didn't want to blunder things up again."

"So we divided up the pie extra carefully."

"And we made sure to count ourselves this time . . ."

"Twice."